THE LAST PRAYER

AARADHANA AGARWAL

Copyright © Aaradhana Agarwal
All Rights Reserved.

ISBN 978-1-68586-506-1

This book has been published with all efforts taken to make the material error-free after the consent of the author. However, the author and the publisher do not assume and hereby disclaim any liability to any party for any loss, damage, or disruption caused by errors or omissions, whether such errors or omissions result from negligence, accident, or any other cause.

While every effort has been made to avoid any mistake or omission, this publication is being sold on the condition and understanding that neither the author nor the publishers or printers would be liable in any manner to any person by reason of any mistake or omission in this publication or for any action taken or omitted to be taken or advice rendered or accepted on the basis of this work. For any defect in printing or binding the publishers will be liable only to replace the defective copy by another copy of this work then available.

Contents

Preface	*v*
Acknowledgements	*vii*
Prologue	*ix*
1. A Perplexed Day	1
2. A Shocking Revealation	8
3. Love In Air	16
4. An Errie Night	23
5. Smriti – A Saviour	30
6. A Horrific Prediction	37
7. The Last Prayer	44
8. A New Beginning	51
Author's Biography	57

Preface

My younger brother Anurag Padia died all of sudden due to cardiac arrest. It was very shocking to the entire family. He was just 39 years old. His untimely death shattered us. He could not achieve what he had aspired for.

His absence has made me write something on people who have a short life and about the pain and suffering of family members. How cruel it is not to get time to fulfill desires and dreams! I have heard Garud Puran and believe what is mentioned in it. It says the soul resides in the house till the completion of all rituals. My story is woven around this fact.

The book is close to my heart as in the main protagonist I have visualized my brother Anurag.

There are 8 chapters in the book that show love, thrill, hope and disappointment in human relationship. How helpless we are in hands of destiny is well projected in the story. I am sure this book will touch the heart of the readers.

Acknowledgements

I am thankful to my parents Shri S.N. PADIA and Smt. USHA PADIA who have taught me simplicity, honesty, and purity of thoughts pave the way to a blessed and peaceful life.

Thanks to my younger brother Kunal Padia who motivates me to grow and learn new things.

I am thankful to my daughter Tisha who has helped me in publishing the book and my husband Ajay who is always supportive in pursuing my dream.

Finally, I am thankful to my brother Anurag who has left behind beautiful memories. The book is dedicated to him.

Prologue

Samar, a young architect has achieved success at a young age. He has the potentiality to turn his dreams into a reality. None can stop him. While running fast on the success path, he gets a major hurdle. His life takes another turn. However, he accepts his destiny and proceeds with absolute peace of mind.

1

A PERPLEXED DAY

Om Bhur Bhuvaḥ Swaḥ, Tat-savitur Vareñyaṃ
Bhargo Devasya Dheemahi,Dhiyo Yonaḥ Prachodayāt

He wakes up at 4.30 AM listening to this holy mantra which pours into his ears by a musical alarm clock. An Ayurvedic ideology says, 'Waking up at Brahma Muhurta keeps a body healthy.' He opens his palms; while looking at them, chants holy mantras, rubs them together, and then feels its warmth on his face. Since his childhood, he pays gratitude to God for gifting a day. Mumbai Sky is dark. During summer, in the island city, the dawn is around 5.35 AM from the Westside window of his bedroom, he greets the full moon which will set in an hour, praises its pristine tranquillity and beauty; and then with a smile gets ready to start a new promising day. He begins his day by jogging in a nearby park at 5 AM 5- 5.30 AM joggers are not present in large numbers. With the rising of the golden crimson sun, health enthusiasts fill the park.

He loves to greet people who join him with full of positive vibes. They welcome each other by exchanging greetings such as Radhe- Radhe, Hari Om, Hare Krishna instead of Good Morning. While walking, many listen to

THE LAST PRAYER

Hindi songs of the golden era on their mobile phones without using earbuds. The music floats in the air and calms everyone's mind. A giant clock at the main gate of the park helps to measure speed. The joggers have their own time slot and the clock doesn't allow them to reduce their pace. By 6 AM the Sun is visible. He welcomes the sun by folding his hands. Early risers have a glimpse of two planetary objects within an hour- the setting moon and the rising sun. He jogs, runs, does limb exercises on gym equipment installed there. One and half hours are enough to spend in the park.

It is in his routine for the last three years to walk and run in the huge park which is adjacent to his posh residential complex. Around a freshwater lake filled with ducks, fish, swans the beautifully maintained park is sprawling over several acres. All the morning walkers of different age groups look so alike in jogging suits and comfortable sports shoes with water bottles in hand. Most people know each other as they meet daily. Members of different clubs such as laughter club, boat club, cricket, badminton, and football club don't break their routine and from 5.30 AM to 9.30 AM the park is fully packed, humming with human bees. They are decent, well-mannered, and focussed on their rigorous exercise and health-maintained activities so that they can reap the benefits of natural surroundings, can inhale fresh oxygen. There is a wife who perhaps doesn't get her husband the whole day, so while walking she blabbers on and on and her husband listens to her patiently and responds by nodding his head.

He is a fitness freak and believes one can live a long healthy life. After spending an hour in the park, he gets ready for his big corporate office where he has been working for the last ten years. He prefers to ignore elevators and use a staircase to reach his office which is on the seventh floor of a thirty-storied skyscraper just to keep himself absolutely fit. Further, to avoid health issues that can be developed due to sitting continuously on a chair for long hours he does light exercises in his cabin. He walks while talking on mobile. His evenings are spent in the gym of his housing complex for a rigorous muscular workout. He is an inspiration for the youth. The ladies cite his examples to motivate their careless husbands. His free consultancy has shaped many obesity-prone people. His well-maintained physique, strict diet regimen; keto diet, serious and dedicated efforts to remain fit have made him an ideal for those who are lazy enough to follow any strict disciplined routine.

However, for the last one month, he has noticed excessive breathing problems because of which he faces difficulty in maintaining the long workout regime. He is just thirty-five so hasn't consulted any doctor as he assumes little rest or a few hours' sound sleep is what he needs. His wife has noticed his increased rate of heartbeat and has cautioned him to be a little slower as his body is not reacting favorably. He ignores her concern by considering it as a normal worry of wife and mother. He suggests her have some peace of mind so that she won't transfer her fear, which is resulted from her overthinking, to him. He can't afford to be sick. Sickness is a luxury for him.

His profession is crucial; it demands his full attention, the highest level of creativity, and a unique way of prompt execution. He is an architectural engineer working in one of the branches of a globally reputed construction company that designs luxurious villas as well as bungalows for the ultra-rich class. Recently he is promoted to a senior architect of the company and is given a big project to show his artistic talent. Handling a team of ten creative minds is very stressful. Opinions differ, creative differences delay the progress of work and as a leader, he has to bear the brunt of senior's frustration regarding the deadline of the project completion. His immediate boss loves to scream, criticize and demotivate. He hates facing him every day but daily reporting about work progress is mandatory as the reputation of the company should not be spoiled.

He is one of the most referred architects of the company. Clients trust him because he understands their vision and presents it on paper exactly by working day and night without any rest. He well dictates his team members how to execute the plan, respects their creative freedom but makes it clear that the final approval will be in his hand. His team has excellent architects, some are juniors and a few are his colleagues. He knows that a wise selection of designs will guarantee the success of the project and will fetch not only promotion but a fat bonus with an increment. So to boost his energy he has begun consuming iron and vitamin capsules as well as has increased intake of protein shakes.

His working hours sometimes get stretched to 18 hours a day. From 9 AM to midnight 3 AM his mind is engaged with the ongoing assignments. A four-hour sound sleep is enough to get him back to his work. Such stressful days can create permanent internal damage to his body system. But he is absolutely ready to sacrifice his comforts. In a corporate world to secure a high post and the trust of the higher authorities is very challenging. There are many hidden competitors who keep an eye on each other's promotion and growth. A little mistake can be projected as a blunder of an employee but success is mostly credited to the immediate boss. His hard sincere work as a team leader or mentor is always under the scanner. The daily update of the running project is silently sucking his stamina. Many a time his dependency on team members is also troubling him.

Unknown to his struggle and stress, his family is proud of his achievements at such a tender age. He has a lavish 3BHK flat in a posh area, a luxurious car, annual membership of a reputed club. All enjoy the amenities, foreign tours, and lavish home parties. For the family members and relatives, he is a money magnet, a wish fulfiller, a person who has the ability to win the entire world. He loves attention, recognition, and flattery. The truth is, however, shocking. It is known to his wife only that he is under heavy debt. He maintains this lifestyle by paying hefty monthly installments against a huge loan granted by a leading bank. The worries are slowly developing symptoms of sleep deprivation. Without sleeping pills, he can't have sound sleep. Too many drugs are his daily requirements to keep him energetic.

One round of the park takes five minutes and he completes six rounds daily. But today he is extremely exhausted after finishing three rounds in fifteen minutes. He tries to push himself but his body denies to support him. Panting heavily, he stops for a while to normalize his fast, uncontrolled breathing. Sweating profusely, he bends half of his body and looks around for any vacant sitting place. Few steps ahead he finds a cemented bench. He sips water, collects his strength, and walks to the seat. It's 6.30 AM. The Sun has spread its aura and enjoying the beautiful welcoming songs of birds. Sitting on the bench he looks at the beauty of the lake and the cheerful activities of water birds. A cool breeze is blowing. In the calm peaceful environment while resting he doesn't know when his eyelids heavy with tiredness are closed. Oh! What is this? In a time of dawn why there is absolute darkness of no moon midnight? Is there a solar eclipse today?

A moment later he feels to be pushed on a dark path? There is no trace of light as if someone has blindfolded him. He is unable to feel and visualize anything but can hear sound. He tries to comprehend his surrounding through the auditory sense. He is clueless why the onlookers present in the park are not protecting him? He may be put inside a big sack and so none can see him. He is scared. After a while, he senses he is no more in the park. Why is he being led to some unknown destination? Is he kidnapped? Oh no! The Ransom amount must be in crores. He has heard about such a gang that is involved in these criminal practices. He calms down his senses and concentrates on what is heard. All of a sudden he hears some familiar sound and soon after that he sees daylight. After regaining his eyesight, he is stress-free. What is this? The presence of a crowd at the main entrance of his housing society frightens him. He enters his home only to be shocked to find an assembly of his relatives and office friends inside. He looks down and spots a body covered in a white sheet lying on the floor. "Oh my God! Who is it? Papa or mom?

"Is it Papa? He was complaining about chest pain the previous night. Oh! When I went out in the morning for jogging he might have taken his last breath. Now I understand why I feel not continuing my exercise. I should return home early. Now, all responsibility of handling family-related issues and the emotional state of the aged mom is mine. How shall I prepare mom to bear this pain?"

He is in deep sorrow. All of a sudden he spots his father crying. His aunt offers him some medicine but he refuses.

"If Papa is alive then whose body is there lying on the floor? Is it Mom? Oh no! She has been suffering from high

BP for the last year. Oh! I should consult a doctor immediately. Oh! No! How can I be bereft of her? Who will now make delicious traditional delicacies and maintain our traditions and family culture? Smriti is not yet perfect in managing all customs. Who will take care of Papa, Sunny, me and Smriti? She should hear the good news that she is going to be a grandmother again." He cries aloud and while wiping tears he finds his mother consoling his father. He is completely shaken in fear. If not she too, then who has left for heavenly abode?

His wife is seen nowhere. His five years old son Sunny is sitting in the living room on the lap of one of his relatives. He looks very confused and is crying. Where is Sunny's mom? How can she leave Sunny alone like this? He can't understand what's going on as a priest is instructing the little child to follow some instructions. He goes inside the bedroom to scold his wife but controls his anger when finds her fainted lying on the bed. She is surrounded by ladies. Mrs. Pujari, the family doctor, is examining her.

2
A SHOCKING REVELATION

People are crying, consoling each other, but Samar's physical presence is ignored by them as if willingly neglecting him. His cousins with whom last night he has planned a trip to Goa are not paying attention to his question. He is asking repeatedly who is lying on the floor but they turn a deaf ear to him. 'What is going on? Are people playing pranks on me?'

His wife regains consciousness after few minutes. The doctor announces nothing to worry about. She is pregnant with a second baby. Oh my God! He is going to be a father again. Wait! That's good news, though the timing of its arrival is not appropriate as someone has died. But why the doctor is looking miserable and the ladies in the room are showing sympathy to his wife? She is also sad. Oh no! What happened! Is she not happy? He rushes to cuddle his wife. "May this time a beautiful girl will be welcomed by us!" he whispers in her ears. He embraces her but she hasn't responded to him. "Hasn't she felt my warm hug?"

In anger, he goes out and sits near the body. His heart is sunk. He goes near to the dead body to have a close view of the face by lifting the white sheet from the face.

"Who can be this? Let me see."

He slowly tries to pull the sheet but is failed.

"What is this? I am unable to touch anything!"

He begins crying. At the same moment, a priest appears there and lifts the white cloth a little bit. Samar is stunned to see the uncovered face of the dead person. He howls loudly.

"How is it possible? How can I be there on the floor when I am watching everyone? How can the body resemble my face exactly? "

He recalls his last moments and murmurs to himself. "In front of the lake, I sat on a bench, closed my eyes for few relaxing moments, just to control my fast breathing. How can that nap turn into my eternal sleep?"

He can't believe that he is dead and it's his body lying on the floor for the last rituals.

Samar hears what the gathering is whispering to one another,

"Few joggers spotted him lying unconsciously." Mr. Madnani utters.

"Yes, as soon as they noticed that Mr. Chakraborty was sleeping on the bench, they informed others." Mr. Kumar confirms.

"We all tried to wake him up but he didn't respond, then Mr. Mehta noticed he was not even breathing." Mr. Rungta with a heavy voice says.

"Mehta was so panic that he cried loudly, "OMG! He is not breathing," adds Mr. Rungta.

"A doctor was present in the park. He read his pulses and declared, "Oh No! He is dead. Perhaps, a massive heart

THE LAST PRAYER

attack!" Mr. Chetan continues.

They inform the family and the body is sent to the nearest hospital where Mr. Chakraborty is known to the staff for being a frequent visitor for a regular health check-up. After examining, the family doctor declares there is no sign of life is seen. Samar has died in the park. He suggests taking the body home.

"How can I die so early? I have always taken good care of my health, never smoked, or have an irregular diet. What will happen to my project, my promotion? In my absence, it will definitely be halted. My untimely death has spoiled everything. My second baby! I won't be known to it. The baby would never have any memory of mine. My Sunny! How will he bear this loss? He is so small and now has to take care of his Mom and later his younger brother or sister. Why have you done this to me, God? My life was promising and I had to shine in the sky of fame. "

He sobs but is unheard.

"How the loan will be paid? Will my family return to the bank my long-cherished dream car and this lovely beautifully decorated flat?" He looks at his parked BMW and roams around his home which are his proud possession, symbols of his success.

"Now the second baby is coming. My family has to curtail the expenses. Papa's irregular income through investment counseling is not enough. How will my family repay loans?"

He spots his subordinates, colleagues, and office staff at his home. Some of his team members Shyam, Neeraj, Shreya, Madan are talking to each other. All look upset and shocked. He reaches near to them to hear their topic of discussion.

10

'Who'll handle now such a big project? Sir shouldn't leave us so early. He was a great architect. There was much to learn from him,' Shyam says.

'Yes, you're right. Let's see who'll be given this project now. I think Madan Sir will be chosen,' Neeraj utters. He continues, "I am afraid if we will get the same creative liberty Samar sir used to give.'

'Madan! Oh no! My biggest rival! Now, he has none to compete with. His progress path is free of hurdles and is clear. Oh, God! Why have you called me so early?' Samar sobs.

His first meeting with Madan as a candidate on the day of the interview in that reputed multinational company flashes in Samar's mind. Both were nervous but cleared the interview round successfully and on joining day were elated to find each other as colleagues. They worked together under the same boss in the same department. Being known to each other since the interview day, they used to spend time together as close buddies.

Samar was known for his unique ideas and to get assured if his idea would be appreciated he always consulted with Madan. Madan never kept him in dark and always provided honest opinions. But this friendly gesture was a big deception. In the appraisal month, Madan was selected for promotion and Samar got just appreciation. He was surprised and to clear his doubt he barged in the boss's cabin and asked how Madan was better than him when in all projects he had executed his unique, out-of-the-box ideas and completed the projects timely.

The boss listened to him and replied, "If you are better than Madan then why is every time you ask for his expert opinion? I have been informed by Madan before your every presentation how he has corrected your silly designs and helped you to make them appropriate. So, it is he who needs to be promoted."

Samar felt as if something very valuable in friendship called Trust had lost its value as it was snatched from him. What a backstabbing, a betrayal in friendship! How conveniently Madan proved himself worthier in front of the boss without making any effort.

Sadly, Madan's fake friendly gesture to guide him in his ideas damaged his image in the first year of the job greatly. However, he decided not to break the friendship as discussing the project in private was his own mistake. He should understand in the competitive world it was foolish to believe colleagues blindly. Further, he learned that any of his friends could do a conspiracy against him to sabotage his reputation.

He still hasn't forgiven Madan for his crafty tricks. In front of the higher authorities, Madan has left no stone unturned in portraying him in a bad light. After the transfer of that boss, Samar is being appreciated as he always presents his ideas in front of everyone during meetings so his contribution can be seen and none can take credit for his efforts. The next year he gets desired long-awaited promotion and equals Madan. He is welcomed heartily by the treacherous friend Madan in the success party, but he never reveals that his trust is already broken and he keeps only a professional relationship with Madan.

While thinking about all these past sad incidents, suddenly, a broad smile appears on Samar's face. He smiles at the thought that now is a soul he can visit anywhere. He instantly enters Madan's house. After having cold water offered by his wife, Madan in a deep shock says to her, 'Samar has always misunderstood me thinking I played dirty office games to prove him unworthy of taking responsibilities. His sudden death hasn't given me time to clear the clouds of negativity. I just wished to say to him there was no fault of mine in the situations when he had faced humiliation.'

'What a great liar!' Samar utters in disgust. The moment he is about to leave Madan's house, a mobile phone rings and Madan picks the phone.

'Yes Sir! YA, I have attended the funeral and have just returned. I get the sad news in the morning. My friend resides in the same locality and he has informed all of us. I am shocked. I can't believe Samar is no more now."

Yes, his five years old son Sunny has done the ritual. Samar is mingled with the five elements of the universe. He is no more part of this worldly life."

Samar notices all of a sudden Madan's face begins sparkling like a diamond. After a few minutes' pause, Samar hears him saying,

"What! Seriously! Are you appointing me as a project head of that prestigious project? Thank you, Sir. I won't disappoint you and late Samar too. May his soul rest in peace!"

'What happened?' Madan's wife asks because a man who has been so broken-hearted a little earlier is so cheerful now. "Have you heard the proverb, Someone's loss is someone's gain?" he asks her.

"Yes, but whose loss, whose gain!" His perplexed wife further questions.

"It's our gain and loss of Samar, the former project head. Oh! What a relief! I don't have to wait for promotion now as Samar, my only competitor is no more. Thank you, God, for being so prompt in listening to my prayer for professional growth." He says joyfully and starts making future plans.

THE LAST PRAYER

Samar can't stay there anymore and returns home. He weeps bitterly.

'Who will take care of my family?' Oh! No, Papa has fainted. I can't do anything." He feels extreme helplessness.

Luckily, after the birth of Sunny, he immediately insured his family. He remembers the day when an insurance advisor Moumita approached him. As an expert financial analyst, she calculated his risks, his future requirements of money for the upbringing of Sunny, his expenses after retirement, and then suggested a term plan at a minimal yearly premium. Smriti also praised him for the right decision.

He now realizes, how important it is to take life cover after embracing parenthood! He sits on a revolving chair in the study room. During the daytime, his father uses the room to meet his clients, and then it is used for his office work till late at night. The room has a huge bookshelf, computer desk, a comfortable sitting arrangement for visitors, and an attached bathroom. Samar knows as soon as the insurance company will get the news of his demise, Moumita will be here. He is eagerly waiting for her arrival.

He has insurance cover of one crore. His wealth creation is done systematically in name of his wife and parents. Unfortunately, investments in their name are in a locking period of five years so the withdrawal of money is chargeable. However, he is relaxed as Smriti knows all of his investments and loans in detail and are well maintained by her. He knows nothing will be wasted and whatever he has accumulated will be multiplied by his intelligent and sensible wife.

That night relatives stay at his home to take care of the family. The next morning, Moumita arrives with a white rajnigandha garland. She pays condolence. After the

14

paperwork, she hands over a cheque of one crore to Smriti. Luckily, he has a joint account with his wife so the money deposited to the account can be used by her without any problem. His family shouldn't be worried about the repayment of huge loans. He is sure that one month's salary and PF amount will be transferred to his account from his office soon.

3
LOVE IN AIR

In the afternoon Samar's family members discuss how to run the house by curtailing household expenses. His mother suggests reducing the number of domestic staff members. But Smriti refuses. They have recently bought BMW on loan. This should be returned to the company but his father disagrees as it's a fulfillment of Samar's long-cherished desire. Sunny's school, Smriti's job and classes will continue as it is. Smriti's brother insists she should be shifted to Kerala as she is pregnant and is going through mental trauma. Smriti suggests selling out their ancestral house which is in their hometown. Mr. Chakraborty's hometown is in the Jharkhand district. Together with a house, he has a shop at the main market of the city. Both are closed as the Chakraborty family has shifted to Mumbai long ago. Maintaining that property is of no use now. So, it is unanimously decided to sell it off. Samar likes the proposal. In Mumbai future of his children is bright.

He looks at Smriti. She is tired, confused, worried and in grief. He feels her joy of having a second child is a little faded now. Now, she must be regretting the decision of having one more child. He just prays child and mother may overcome this trauma and a healthy baby is born. He is feeling heavy-hearted and silently watching the last rituals. The family has chosen one of his best pictures to display in the living room. All his favorite dishes are being prepared to feed a Brahmin boy. His clothes and foot wares have been donated to needy people. Smriti is handling entire arrangements silently. She is advised to have a proper meal. Her parents and brother provide emotional strength to the grieved family.

Samar's father informs the Club about Samar's demise and requests to cancel the membership. The Goa trip is slashed too. Samar is helplessly watching and realizing the worthless, cynical chase towards fame and money. He raises his hands up and in loud voice cries out, "I know death is inevitable but God why without any warning or hint it happens."

Samar feels sorry for Smriti. He remembers how much his parents initially judged his decision of marrying a South Indian girl. They declared her unsuitable for the family because of her different culture and were worried about how she would adjust to a Bengali family. But now they are highly happy and content with her and are proud of his decision. In his close and distant family, everyone wishes daughter-in-law like Smriti.

His love story is so enthralling that he is asked several times by his cousins and friends to narrate about their first meeting, initial uncertainties, doubts, hurdles in detail. He enjoys living those moments again and again. Smriti's face turns red in shyness when in front of relatives when he starts unveiling their sweet moments. But she enjoys the way he narrates them. She feels as if she is his muse and he is creating a piece of poetic art. At present, there is nobody around Samar to ask for it but he wishes to tread down memory lane. Sitting on the chair he begins recalling the first encounter with his sweetheart.

Meeting Smriti in an engineering college on 10[th]July never seems to be turned into a successful love affair at the first time. Smriti, a fresher, two years junior to him, captures Samar's heart instantly. One fine sunny morning, after two consecutive days of incessant rain, brings a smile to everyone and all are ready to reach their workplace by enjoying sun-kissed Nature's beauty. He too leaves for college. Two days of home arrest has irritated him. News of deluge in low lands, damage of property is highly pathetic. He decides to visit those areas with food packets, clothes and medicine. He has made a plan how to collect all these and help the needy. He will involve professors and administrators to raise money and medical aids.

A crowd of confused new joiners creates noise in the silent atmosphere of the college vicinity. When he is about to enter the lift, a group of fresher stops him to ask the way to their classroom as they have seen only the college office. Being a senior he throws attitude and simply ignores them. The other reason is on the first day of the third year he doesn't want to be late for lectures. He makes excuses but they request again. He quenches their query and a girl in pink suit thanks him with a sweet smile. He notices her innocent face, long hair, light kajal, a beautiful hand-embroidered cloth bag on one shoulder. She instantly steals his heart. He nods his head with a smile and moves ahead. That lovely face and the sweet voice have made his day. His friends try to find the reason for his happiness, but he keeps them in darkness.

After a week, Samar spots Smriti in the library. She is there to do some formalities to get issued a library card. Her pleasant persona creates a happy atmosphere and that day he knows her surname. She is Smriti Iyer. The librarian Ma'am Smt. Usha Mathur likes her pleasant personality and sober mannerism very much. She hands her over the library card, some suggestions and extra information. As Samar is a bookworm and loves to spend time with books in that premise, she all of a sudden calls his name and commands, 'Samar, meet Smriti. Do help her in finding books and if she needs to help her in making notes.' She then turned to Smriti and uttered, "Samar is a very studious and intelligent student. He is very helpful too. Whenever you find me busy with other students or in office work, you can take his help." With the same killing smile, Smriti nods her head like an obedient girl.

Since that day, Samar and Smriti begin meeting frequently. Sometimes in the canteen, in the recreation room, and in the library, of course, they are seen together. Her most appealing quality is her love for literature as if by default she has joined engineering. She belongs to a family where all love writing. So expressing her thoughts and feelings through words is in her genes. She loves to remain silent. Whenever Samar asks anything she looks somewhere at a distance as if she thinks how to reply in an impressive way. Her beautiful eyes begin twinkling, her lips open a little when in a soft voice answers the query. He visualizes himself as her worshipper who is standing in front of his idol by forgetting the surrounding.

Her traditional outfit, minimal makeup, shoulder-length well-combed pinned hair, and glow of intelligence on her face makes him crazy. They both love to participate in cultural programs and sports activities. She is excellent in dance, singing and can enact any character very well. Her communication skill is impressive too. In group discussion professors and participants love to hear her speech. She always has rebellious fiery statements in favor of downtrodden and under-privileged people. Her active involvement in all social activities makes her popular in the college.

Samar books his place in her heart after a year. His unconditional love and support she appreciates and realizes he is the one with whom she can spend her entire life. Their family knows about their friendship so they are invited to each other's house on special occasions like anniversaries, birthdays, festivals and religious functions. She relies on him and without having a discussion with him, she never gets involved in any college activity that is completely new. Her parents are delighted to have Samar as her guiding star. He too protects her from many lustful, jealous, and furious eyes.

Samar is an active member of a village development organization formed by the founder of the college. Every year the members visit villages and inspect the infrastructure there. The engineers try to resolve issues and provide technical help. They use donation money to help the needy. She too wishes to join them and expresses her desire to be part of one such program. She fills the form and after an interview to check her sincerity she is selected. The village chosen is Mangalajodi, a fishing village globally known as The Bird's Paradise, situated on the banks of Odisha's Chilika lake. She is so excited as it's an older village that hosts more than 1.5 lakhs of migratory birds between November to March. The village is a global wetland habitat and is declared an International Bird Conservation Area.

She joins the group. The tour is for one week and includes activities like meeting with the village head to explain developments in the fishing field, new instruments, techniques and marketing strategy. Smriti adds a new point to promote the village as an educational tourist spot under ecotourism. The villagers are happy with the idea of getting students in peak season. Bird lovers, nature admirers, children can acquire knowledge of birds, their migratory patterns, and breeding cycles. They will get inspired by knowing how the villagers, who were earlier poachers, become protectors of birds.

They stay in a big guest house of eleven rooms which is on the outskirts of the village. There are arrangements for girls and boys separately. There are arrangements for a bonfire, musical night and story-telling. Every night after having dinner all of them showcase their talents. The best of the activities is a narration of the horror story. Being science students it is fun to cook ghost stories whose existence is never to be believed by them. While cooking stories the storyteller gets inspired by whatever is watched in movies, read in books and heard by people. The narration style brings fun, excitement and sometimes scary feeling. Samar and Smriti don't trust in any supernatural entity. They laugh while listening to such incidents. They try their best to educate people who are affected by the tricks of Tantrik who befool them and rob them.

One evening after having dinner at 8 PM. Samar and Smriti go out to chill together while their friends decide to relax in the rooms. By that time the entire locality is in deep silence. Street lamp posts are insufficient to light properly the roads. Villagers are at their cottages as they are not habituated to staying out of home till late hours. The couple carries their mobile phones to use their torchlight. There is a beautiful pond at a distance of a five-minute walk. Holding each other's hands, they are proceeding towards the pond in the cool tranquil full moon night. The atmosphere is so romantic that Smriti starts humming an old classic Hindi Bollywood Lata Mangeshkar's song that creates magic. Wow! So sweet and silky her voice is! He requests her to sing properly so that he can record the song in her voice. She agrees but with a condition. As it is a duet song, he too has to join her. He gladly accepts the proposal. They both get immersed in the world of music.

They are warned not to go near the pond as nocturnal animals can attack. In the complete moonlit night, they can be spotted by the animals who appear there to quench their thirst. If they sense the presence of humans, they can attack. A shrill hooting sound of an owl makes Smriti hold Samar's arm tightly. He too doesn't disappoint her; he encircles his arm around her waist to give assurance that in his presence her safety is guaranteed. The pond is dimly lit because of a tiny Shiva temple nearby. It is a famous temple where wishes are fulfilled. People from around the corners visit there. The temple doors are shut and the area is no more buzzing with the devotees and priests. They sit on a steel bench under a lamp post and cherishing the moment of togetherness. They have decided to offer prayers before leaving the village. Samar is sure he will ask God for granting Smriti as his wife. He is hopeful nothing will go unfavorable to him.

4

AN ERRIE NIGHT

While resting on Samar's shoulder Smriti closes her eyes. He can feel that her feelings for him are soft, deep, and clear. He dreams of having a family with her. He knows he is a one-woman man. She will never regret her decision of marrying him. If he wins her heart, he will never be distracted by any other attractive girl. He'll remain a loyal husband and a responsible father. He'll not be a dictator and give her space and freedom. He'll be with her in all highs and lows. After doing the job for few years, he will start his own manufacturing unit to provide a luxurious life to her. He will never doubt her and prove himself the best choice for him.

He feels so comfortable in her presence, nothing to be ashamed of. Love has blossomed in his heart and its fragrance will definitely bring her near to him. He asks if she is feeling sleepy.

"No, I am just enjoying the quietness of the night with you."

He is elated to get this reply. He opens his heart saying she is the first girl in his life with whom he is spending a night under the starry sky. None has captured his attention earlier the way she has done. He is glad to have such a multi-talented friend. She smiles. Her eyes are still closed as if she is not ready to break the continuity of this moment. Her silence is encouraging him to vent out his feelings. He doesn't disclose much of the future plans he has just made. He is afraid if she takes it in a wrong way because from the deepest core of his heart he wishes her to be with him as his life partner.

This heavenly moment gets disturbed when Smriti hears a sound. She opens her eyes and gets startled finding a shadow throwing a stone into the water body. She rushes to the spot with Samar and in the light of the mobile phones, they notice a girl is planning to jump into the water. They instantly raise an alarm. Being frightened she stops and looks at them angrily. They are shocked when instead of being grateful to them, she shouts, "Why do you trouble me? I am here to end my miserable life."

They calm down her and request her to sit on the bench. In the street light, she is clearly visible. In front of them, there is a beautiful teenage village girl clad in a red-bordered white sari. Her entire face is red with anger. After few minutes she gains control of her fast, irregular breathing. They talk to her gently, enquire about her whereabouts. Asking about her suicidal attempt, an extreme decision of ending life she prefers to maintain silence. She refuses to reveal the reason. Smriti sits beside her and like a mature caring person utters, "You don't have to get scared of us. We are engineering college students, halted in the guest house for a week. We're here to resolve the problems of villagers through modern techniques. We won't share your secret with anyone as we don't know you and any of your family members. You can take our help without any hesitation." We have carried a water bottle with us, so offer her some water. She rejects the offer.

"Sure, you won't say anyone about my suicidal attempt", she asks in a low voice.

"Yes, you can rely on us," They both promise her together.

A nervous village girl in such a vulnerable state after much thinking decides to open her heart in front of her saviors. She says she is madly in love with a boy of another caste but her parents are against this match. She has overheard their plan of sending her to a distant relative house in another village so that they can get her married forcibly.

Smriti asks, "Are you educated?"

She answers till the primary level she has studied and then loses her interest in bookish knowledge. She belongs to the fishermen community and is interested in weaving fishing nets.

"Why don't you protest? You can convince them." Samar asks.

"I decide to elope. To discuss the future plans I meet my boyfriend but he refuses to support me. "

The next shocking revelation is her pregnancy which she has discovered two months earlier and in the morning when she informs her boyfriend, he immediately breaks a three-year relationship by denying the child's responsibility. She has no other option so plans to end her life to make him realize her value.

After narrating her side of the story she feels relaxed and has controlled her sobbing and hiccupping. She is about to leave the place when Samar asks if she would mind giving them the name and address of the boy so they can help her in that critical time. She looks at him with utter disbelief. He doesn't know what makes her believe him, she utters her boyfriend's name and address. Initial of his name is inscribed on her arm beautifully. The address is said verbally which is easy to remember.

The next morning in the guest house they call Subbu, a boy of twenty-four years old. He arrives. His appearance is so weird and unimpressive that they can't help but build a negative opinion about him. How blind love has ruined once again an innocent life! His tight jeans and t-shirt, goggles on his face, red-colored lips due to betel juice, and arrogant attitude show how selfish careless guy he is! He can never be serious about maintaining the dignity of lady love and be ready to fight for asking approval of their love by facing the wrath of society. It is clearly seen that the girl has overlooked his negative traits and that's the reason why her parents are against her. She becomes a victim of love, is destined to suffer alone as the boy is a completely useless, uneducated, and irresponsible person. Samar and Smriti in stern voices ask if he knows Fulwa. He reacts at the name shockingly as if he has touched some live electric wire. With wide opened eyes in reply, he puts a question about how they know her.

Smriti wishes to explain how they have met her at night near the pond and she herself has narrated all that is done to her. But she doesn't reveal anything. He cannot believe that the city dwellers are aware of the dark secret of his relationship. However, noticing the truth in their voice, he accepts his mistake of denying responsibility. He says, "Four years ago they were madly in love but unexpected news of her pregnancy shook him badly. I wanted to get rid of the child but she was adamant about entering into parenthood. She forced me to marry in the temple and if parents would not accept them then to elope, but I couldn't gather the courage."

Samar interrupts by saying if he wishes they can help him getting settled down with Fulwa in the city.

He replies, "How can it be? Even God can't do this."

Samar and Smriti create an opinion he may be engaged with someone else.

Smriti asks, "Do you love someone else?"

He answers, "No, I am not engaged with anyone. But how can I marry Fulwa who has committed suicide last year? In front of my eyes, she jumped into the pond. I knew swimming so I tried to pull her out but she vanished. Her post-mortem report declared her pregnancy and since then I am in deep trouble. Nobody knows in the village that I am the reason for her parent's grief, I am the father of her unborn child. People curse her and declare her as unchaste. I feel guilty but can't say the truth as in our village punishment for such an act is very harsh."

Now it is their turn to be shocked. Smriti's face turns pale in fear. Samar commands the boy to leave the place without answering how they come to know about his secrets which are buried with the death of his girlfriend. He returns as a confused and frightened person. After some time, they both decide to meet Fulwa's parents. They are in deep agony after losing their only child. When they come to know how Fulwa has narrated her story to them, they begin crying. They curse themselves as unconsciously they are the reasons for her suicide. Smriti consoles them and asks them to perform the last rituals so that her soul can rest in peace. They inform how Subbu is ready to declare himself as her husband and father of the child. They discuss with the temple priest how to provide peace to the restless soul of Fulwa. The next morning, they visit the Shiva temple and offer money to the priest to perform puja for the peace of Fulwa's soul. Subbu with his parents attend the puja and since that day none spot Fulwa at night near the pond.

The horrifying event of meeting with Fulwa's spirit and organizing puja after settling down issues with the villagers, Fulwa's parents, and her boyfriend bring Samar and Smriti very close to one another. They share the incident of an encounter with a soul and how they help it resting in peace with friends and family members. They establish the fact that there is an existence of supernatural beings. What our ancient scriptures say about them is all true. It's important to do the last rituals properly so that the dead can leave the mortal world permanently.

After spending few days with Smriti in the village Samar realizes she is a beauty with a brain. Her intuition and emotional intelligence will never betray her. She can save herself from dangers. She is strong enough to stand against brutal love incidents. Soon she imprints her impression on every heart in the college. A month had passed to their visit to the village in Odisha. They are so much in sync with each other but still, he is unsure about her feelings for him. He doesn't know if she has accepted him as a best friend or desires to spend her entire life with him. He is ready to declare his love for her but is scared of losing the precious friendship due to any stupidity. He decides to wait a little more and remains her pillar of support. Hiding of love for her has become so difficult for him. He has nightmares of losing her. He has lost his sound sleep which results in inattentiveness to his studies. If he doesn't receive her calls and messages instantly, he gets worried for her safety.

Smriti too feels special for Samar. He is her dream man who has the power to calm down a stormy ocean. Samar is Smriti's Lord Shiva. She is so secure in his company. In the village, she has realized none but he can only be gifted by God as her life partner. She is just waiting for his love proposal.

In few days Samar becomes so restless that he decides not to suffer anymore silently. One evening he asks what kind of life partner she is dreaming of. She immediately answers a person who can understand her completely and be supportive even if he has doubts in his mind about the success in her chosen path. He must allow her to grow independently and come to the rescue when it is asked.

Samar smiles and asks, "What do you think about me? Do I have all the qualities that you are looking for in your future husband?"

She laughs heartily and utters, "Yes".

That golden moment has ultimately arrived for which they have been waiting for a long time. He is elated to find she has accepted that between them there is something more than friendship. On his farewell day, he proposes to her. She readily agrees. They decide to tie a nuptial knot after acquiring a professional degree and getting a high salaried job. They haven't yet revealed to their parent's seriousness of their relationship but it is known to them what is the importance of their presence in one another's life.

5

SMRITI – A SAVIOUR

---❤️---

Samar and Smriti's long five-year courtship period is amazing. Samar finds in Smriti a friend, a guide, and a mentor. She is so clear-minded that with her he can share everything. They both know exactly what is their goal in life. They are creating a precious eternal bonding. He can never forget the compatibility test incident taken by their friends. Both are surprisingly correct in answering questions based on each other's favorite color, song, person, and moment. Luckily, they have similar ways of solving any problem.

One morning Smriti informs Samar that she will not be in the town as Megha her cousin sister is found dead in a mysterious condition and so she is visiting her residence in Asansol. The incident is highly unfortunate for just a week before they have celebrated Megha's first wedding anniversary. In the anniversary celebration pictures, the couple is looking so much in love with each other. None can imagine that destiny has other plans and the pair is soon to be separated forever.

Megha dies due to a fall from the terrace. She is pushed or it's a suicide, the investigating agency is finding. Her sudden demise has created so much misunderstanding between her parents and in-laws. None are in a healthy mental state in the presence of media and police. In a small town, the news has spread like fire in a forest. Her in-laws had shut them inside their house as they are fed up with being accused. Her husband Mayur is facing the questions of the police knowingly well that he has no proof to prove how much he and his entire family love the deceased. Smriti is close to her sister so she is at her in-laws' house during the last rituals. She is in deep grief and finds it difficult to believe that her beautiful sister Megha is no more.

Megha was a talented, energetic, and extremely beautiful lady of twenty-four years old. She obtained her degree in mechanical engineering, was a trained kathak dancer, and was an amateur writer too. Both Smriti and Megha had spent their entire childhood together. They lived in a big joint family, studied in the same school and college. They had the same friend circle, shared all secrets of life, and never let one another down by revealing the hidden truth to anyone. Their all first experiences of sad, happy, embarrassing, scary, adventurous, naughty, guilty, moments were treasured as precious memories.

The past memories begin troubling Smriti when she sees Megha lying on a floor. She can't forget the blessed married life of her sister. How happy Megha was when she met Mayur in a family get-together which was arranged in a five-star hotel. With the consent of family members, both Megha and Mayur met alone in a café which was in one of the best malls in the city. She was with her aunt. Dressed in a bottled green gown she reached the café on the second floor. She dialed his number and heard a voice, You're looking gorgeous." She turned her face back and found Mayur smiling. In blue jeans and half cotton shirt, he was giving tough competition to her in a matter of appearance. They set facing each other. Both were unable to hide the feeling that they fell in love at first sight.

Megha's aunt was busy with shopping and they were left alone to exchange their thoughts and soft feelings for one another. Mayur made it clear that he had no problem if she wished to do a job. He was happy to get a mechanical engineer as a wife. It was an arranged marriage but an entry of love on the first meeting turned it into a love cum arranged marriage. Megha always had deep love and respect for him. After marriage, on every occasion, she loved to share with everyone how blessed she was for having open-minded in-laws and a husband.

Smriti goes to Megha's room after taking permission from Mayur. It is so beautifully arranged and decorated. The wall pictures of the couple's happy moments create a romantic aura. Every corner of the room has Megha's artistic expression. Smriti is amused to see the artifacts which display the rich taste of the couple. While watching Megha's book collection she notices a blue-golden diary on a bookshelf. She opens it as she has the right to know all secrets of her sister. She can't hold her tears when notices the last diary entry is of that fatal day, just a few hours before her death.

Megha was in habit of noting down all her thoughts and feelings. The diary is her secret sharing medium. She was excellent at creating affirmative quotes. Smriti reads, "It's a lovely sunny morning. Today is an auspicious day to declare what surprise I have stored for my lovely husband and his parents. I can imagine their expression. Mayur will be first shocked to hear that I am going to bring a new life to this world. My in-laws will be overjoyed as they will get a baby to play with it. I just can't wait to see them dancing with joy."

Smriti begins crying knowing about the loss of not only her sister but an expecting mother. It's a huge loss. None can believe a story of a loving couple who would soon be parents has ended in a tragic way. She informs the investigating officer about the diary entry. The angle of torture and murder is dismissed. The diary is submitted as a piece of evidence. However, everyone is in deep grief and inconsolable. News of Megha's pregnancy will be received in this way after her death is beyond imagination.

Smriti can't bear this painful sight and goes to the terrace. She spots few bungalows adjacent to Megha's duplex bungalow. In one of the bungalows, a boy of around seven years is playing with a ball on the terrace. Smriti spots the installation of a CCTV camera on the terrace of that bungalow facing Megha's residence. She immediately calls the officer and he quickly checks the footage of that morning. What a pity! Megha is seen on the terrace doing her morning exercise. Later, she waters the plants. Around 9 o'clock she is seen offering water to Lord Sun. At that moment she turns her head and looks towards a tree. A ball is stuck in one of its branches near to a bird's nest. As the tree is just an arm away from Megha. At the child's request, she tries to release the ball by holding the railing of the terrace. She lifts her up a little more and at the same moment, she feels dizziness due to pregnancy. She loses her control and falls down. It is an accident.

The officer praises Smriti to bring the real incident to light. He also thanks her for saving the family from the wrong accusations. Smriti stays there for fifteen days. For Mayur and his parents, she is an angel sent by God to protect them from lifelong guilt and humiliation. Smriti's parents are proud of her daughter. Smriti with tear eyed silently looks at Megha's huge portrait. She utters, "You need not worry anymore. Your sweetheart Mayur and in-laws are saved. None can harass them. "

Being highly impressed by the incident of Smriti's maturity in handling the sensitive issue I congratulate her and narrate it to my parents and announce she will be their daughter-in-law. They are extremely relaxed to know such an intelligent and brave girl will be their son's wife. After few months without any objection from our parents, her name is officially registered not only in my heart but in all documents as my legal wife. She is now Smriti Iyer Chakraborty. She hasn't changed her surname to announce the union of North and South India.

Smriti enters a new life. In this post-married life, she has moved to Samar's home where she needs to adjust to few things. She is a pure vegetarian and in Samar's family without meat and fish daily meal is incomplete. As Samar's parents know all about her food habits, a separate corner in the kitchen is made to cook non - veg items, and utensils are also kept separately for the purpose. Marriage for them is an amalgamation of two families and they all are elated to experience the vastness of culture and tradition. On a nuptial night, Smriti and Samar vow that they will respect both cultures and raise their children without any pressure to follow one particular family tradition. The cultural and religious issues will be handled with maturity without any superiority complex. They will be faithful to each other; to live a transparent life they'll neither hide nor hesitate to share any embarrassing moment; like best friends listen to each other patiently and then come to conclusion; they will respect the privacy of one another and if they fight, the next morning will be a new day with no bitterness of yesterday.

Next week, they are on a honeymoon trip. Their passion to explore India's ancient culture in archaeological destinations leads them to a UNESCO World Heritage Site Hampi- a city in Karnataka. Near the Tungabhadra river, the city is mentioned in Ramayana and Puranas. It is famous for its ruins belonging to the erstwhile medieval Hindu kingdom of Vijaynagar. The temples of Hampi, its monolithic sculptures and monuments, attract the traveler because of their excellent craftsmanship. They both visit the city during the off-season to avoid the unwanted glares of onlookers at tourist spots. In the less crowded city, they can enjoy togetherness. They stay there in a riverside hotel. They visit the Vittala Mandir to listen to the music of the SAREGAMA pillars which they produce when are tapped delicately.

In Hazara Ram temple they have goosebumps to see fossils that are claimed to be present in the era of Ram and Krishna. In the Virupaksha Temple, they get the blessing of a baby elephant in form of a kiss after giving it a one-rupee coin. The use of a snake as a rope to tie Lord Ganesh's belly so that it won't explode is an interesting story depicted in form of a Ganesha statue whose four hands hold a noose, broken tusk, modak, and a goad. One early morning while offering puja to a famous temple they notice a saint, in his mid- forty, is chanting mantras and sprinkling holy water on the deity. They decide to ask few questions about his life when they see he has a number of followers who are waiting for him to preach a sermon. After half an hour of performing daily rituals while worshipping God, he begins enlightening others with his knowledge of spirituality. Greeting him with respect, they ask for his permission to have a small conversation. He agrees.

After completing his interaction with the disciples, he invites the couple to his room. It is a small clean area with one bed at the corner and a wooden closet to keep the necessary articles. One of the walls is adorned with framed pictures of Lord Shiva, on another wall, there is a wooden hook to hang his Holy yellow cloth which he uses to cover the upper part of his body. They sit on a floor mat. He blesses them for their happy marital life but surprisingly hasn't uttered, "Sada Suhagan Raho" which means 'May your husband be alive in your entire lifetime!"

Smriti doesn't take it lightly. She has heard that the saints have the capacity of predicting the future. Whatever they say, deep meaning is always present. She determines to ask the reason behind it.

She is cautious not to make him angry so begins the conversation with a question, "What has made you follow sainthood?"

He smiles and answers, "A trail of incidents move my heart and I lose my interest in this worldly life."

On request, he narrates some childhood occurrences that have brought a huge transformation in his life and turns him into a saint.

6

A HORRIFIC PREDICTION

At the age of twelve Shambhu, the saint had to share his parent's love with an orphanage rescued by them from a mad dog who was about to devour his soft body. The infant was staying with them and demanded much attention. Shambhu was feeling neglected so one day he planned to get rid of the kid. He took him deep inside a nearby forest and left there. He returned home and was scared to find his parents searching the tiny tot crazily. Many villagers were gathered there. He couldn't lie when was asked about the child. He confessed that he had left the infant in the jungle. Everybody rushed to the place where he had kept the child. Luckily, nothing happened to that child, he was however punished for the inhuman act.

His cruelty was evident. He was proved a selfish boy having no compassion for the dependents. So, on that same day, his parents commanded him to serve his octogenarian grandparents who were completely bedridden. Earlier, they were under the care of his parents but with the arrival of the child, their responsibilities multiplied. So they engaged

Shambhu to stay with the old couple the whole day helping them doing their day-to-day activities. He had to wake up very early in the morning for their cleaning, feeding, and nursing. Twice a day in the morning and evening he had to read holy scriptures for them. Together with this, he had to manage his school study. He skipped his meals many times in a year, always felt himself in a cage, and consequently grew as a restless, impatient teenager. He couldn't rebel because his parents were very strict and never allowed him to neglect his duties.

With much courage one day he requested them to release him from this task. That evening he was explained how his grandparents protected him when he was just born, how his parents sacrificed their comforts to raise him. He was a premature baby and the midwife declared he would not survive even for a day. His grandfather used to bring herbs and skin of medicinal trees from the forest and his grandmother prepared herbal oil to massage him. He was very weak so she fed him by squeezing milk inside his mouth. Due to their efforts, the prediction of a midwife turned wrong. His father asked if he had not been treated kindly, how could he survive in this world? He understood the value of mercy, love, and care. Since then he had been associated with several social activities and experienced real happiness.

His grandparents always desired to attain salvation. They explained to him the greatness of the city Varanasi where the Almighty grants liberation from the cycle of birth and death. They were too weak to travel, He went to Kashi and brought holy Ganga water. He was so fascinated by the city that he planned to stay there permanently. A desire to serve God arose in his heart since then and he began spending his time with spiritual gurus, leaders who led him on the path of Spirituality. This was a matter of concern for his parents. They never wanted him to live a saintly life. The only solution to this problem was his marriage. He was then just fifteen years old. One day after being pressurised to get married, he escaped from his home and joined a group of holy saints. By that time his grandparents were not alive, so he had no reason to live with his parents. He left the village giving the responsibility of them to his brother.

Smriti asks if he has ever visited his parents. He answers, "They are hurt for my elopement but forgive me as I have done this before tying the nuptial knot. I visit my parents, my adopted brother, and his family twice a year."

Smriti and Samar are astonished by the saint's story. How a jealous boy completely transforms into a holy saint!

Shambhu thus slowly gets inclined towards spiritualism since his boyhood. The creation of the universe, God's excellent management, registration of good and bad acts, rewards and punishment he learns through various mythological stories. He takes a pause and says that with the saints he has traveled the entire India and a few years ago get settled in Hampi.

Smriti and Samar stay there for an hour and before leaving Smriti asks the saint why he hasn't uttered 'Sada Suhagan Raho' while pouring his blessings on them, knowing well that they are a newly-wed couple and in India, these words coming out from a saint matters a lot. He tries to avoid the question but she insists.

Samar also asks out of curiosity, "You're hesitating. Do you have the power to see the future?"

He looks at Samar by fixing his eyes deeply on his forehead and utters, "Your life is short but very successful. You will provide your family immense comforts but you won't live long. "

Smriti tries to control her tears ready to roll down on her cheek. She asks, "Is there any way of saving him from the ill luck?"

The Saint thinks a while and nods his head left and right signaling 'no'. But after taking a few seconds' pauses he says to Samar, "You are a pious soul. So in your entire lifetime, God will grant you a special favor. Whatever you ask, God will offer you but only once. Be wise while using the opportunity."

The couple touches his feet and comes out. Both are scared, speechless, and in unrecoverable shock. They regret why they showed interest in knowing the uncertain future. What does the saint mean by short life? That night is the longest night for them. Samar holds Smriti's hand and in deep frustration says, "I am so sorry to make your life miserable. I have never been told even by my parents that my life is short. They don't believe in horoscope and astrology so none know about this truth. I have vowed never to leave you but destiny has a different story to tell."

Smriti consoles Samar who is completely broken not because of the Shocking prediction of his early death but for his soon to be shattered dreams of enjoying longer a happy married life, raising children, and grow old with Smriti. Smriti says, "Love is eternal. Though we'll not be together physically, our souls are ever united. My life is nothing without you. But destiny can't be changed. The saint hasn't mentioned any particular age. So, let's don't take the stress. Be positive and live life normally forgetting all about this prediction."

He wipes his tears and agrees with her. However, both lose interest in staying at that place anymore. Samar is scared. His married life has just started and he, an unfortunate one, comes to know how short-lived all that happiness is. They cut short the travel plans. Both are in a perplexed state of mind. Smriti offers prayers to the temples the next day and they return to their home. They never discussed anything with their parents regarding the prediction of the saint and tried to behave normally but that hidden fear is troubling both of them. They daily wish what the saint has foretold may prove wrong.

Since that incident, Samar is focused on his health. Proper diet, regular health check-ups, no late-night parties, and many other rules he has made for himself. Smriti is worried to see his craziness. She knows too much worry will do more harm than good to his health. She needs him to concentrate on other aspects of life. If she can divert his attention from the short life prediction, he can enjoy his life fully with happiness and peace of mind. She gives him a piece of golden advice. "When you know time is short why don't you plan your life? Think about your career, dreams, and purpose in life. Live life fully." He agrees and since then his goal is to achieve more in less time.

They start investing money in various investment plans. He switches to a high salaried job and tries to achieve targets in the office. His wife being solid rock support opens her own coaching class as well as works in an engineering college as an assistant professor. They both accumulate wealth to afford a comfortable and luxurious life. The parents are extremely happy to see the rapid progress and bless them to be successful in all endeavors. They are unaware of the untold fearful reason for running frantically behind success and wealth.

They are so engrossed in their activities that the decision of entering into parenthood is being postponed by them. In fact, they avoid bringing a new life in this world as they know Smriti has to raise children singlehandedly. Their parents refuse to interfere in their personal life but destiny is always ready to surprise. They receive what they are destined to. One morning Smriti announces three magical words, "We are pregnant." By that time, they have their own big luxurious home, an expensive car, and domestic staff at home. Therefore, the news is pleasant. The child is welcomed grandly. Sunny, his son, completes the family.

"Everything in my life was so perfect then why God you have alienated me from my family." Samar is sobbing. He goes to the living room, the priest is explaining Garud Puran - a conversation between Lord Vishnu and Garud about death, soul, and reincarnation. He sits there folding his legs as if people can watch him. With little interest, he begins listening to it. The priest is saying, 'the distance between the Earth and Yamloke will be covered by the soul in eleven months. Daily 3000 km traveling is required...

The doorbell rings, he rushes to the door.

"Oh my God! Mayur is there to attend the condolence meet. After such a long gap! Death of Megha has broken connection from Mayur's family." Even on the marriage of Samar and Smriti, none from his family are invited. "How has he come to know about the grief of the family?" Samar is managing the traffic of thoughts in his mind.

Mayur humbly greets Samar's parents with folded hands and bows in front of his garlanded picture in reverence. He hasn't met Samar personally but has heard about him from Megha's parents. Smriti comes out from the room as soon as she hears someone from her parent's family has come. She is also equally surprised at his arrival. Samar's parents are not acquainted with Mayur so he is introduced by Smriti as Megha's husband because they only know about Megha. Samar's and Mayur's families never have visited each other's houses as both live in separate cities. Whenever there is any occasion in Smriti's family she only attends the event because Samar has never been granted leave for more than two days from the office. Therefore, he is a stranger to Samar's parents.

Mayur can't speak anything when Smriti greets him as he has gone through the pain resulted from the separation of his life partner. In that room among all relatives, he is the only one who can relate to Smriti's sorrow. He looks at Smriti who once has saved his life and family's honor. How destiny has turned an epitome of courage into a vulnerable person! She is commanding the cook to prepare lunch for the priest and with Sunny trying to behave as a normal being.

Mayur hasn't remarried. He has lost interest in entering into a relationship once again. He denies any kind of emotional bonding. The sudden demise of his wife has shattered him completely. Five years have been passed but Megha's memories are still fresh. He is unable to forget his lovely wife. After Megha's death, Mayur shifts to the Canadian branch of his company because of his parents' pressure to get settle down once again. He doesn't have any child so none object to marry him. But he rejects all proposals. Mayur is a CEO of a telecom company, a globe trotter, has properties in and out of the country, and can provide everything that a woman expects from her spouse. Many relatives have tried to convince him to marry a lady of their choice, but he is adamant. He wishes the same care, love, and support that he has received from Megha.

7
THE LAST PRAYER

A week earlier he has come to India to visit his parents. One day while working on a laptop his phone rings. He picks it up. It is Megha's father who invites him to his place for dinner. He with his parents joins them. During a conversation, he gets the shocking news. He doesn't know how to react to that. Smriti's husband has died! Cardiac arrest at such a young age! Oh! So unfortunate! He must visit her and console her. He knows how much someone is needed at that time when you are left alone by your spouse forever. He consults with his parents. They immediately allow him.

Samar's parents are highly impressed by Mayur to see how he is trying to soothe their saddened hearts. With his decent mannerism, consoling words spoken in a soft voice, assisting Smriti in her activities, he has become their favorite, a close family member. Samar too is glad that Mayur is bringing normalcy in the home. His presence brings a smile to Smriti's face. She has started having fruits and proper meals as there is a new life growing inside her. Sunny is enjoying Mayur's company. On his laptop, he loves to play educational games and in the evening they all have pleasant times. Papa has begun watching television after a week, mummy is extra careful in handling household chores as Smriti needs emotional and moral support. Mayur stays in Smriti's house for two days. On the day of his departure, Samar's papa asks him why he is not marrying again. With a smile, he replies by fixing his eyes on Smriti, "If I find someone like Megha, I would definitely tie the knot again." Samar's mummy follows his fixed eyes on Smriti and takes no time to understand what he means to say. But the situation is not so favorable for such conversation so she ignores what she has comprehended. Samar notices the changed facial expression of mummy but cannot make out why she suddenly changes the topic and asks Mayur about his career and other details.

After returning from Samar's house Mayur is lost. He cannot focus and is inattentive to his work. Smriti's memories have captured his heart. He is unable to think of anything else than her. She is in his mind 24/7. One day he feels lonely and begins watching a video of his wedding. His eyes get fixed on Smriti. He has never paid close attention to her earlier. Smriti has attended his marriage for a short duration due to her college exam. On the occasion of Sangeet, her recitation of a self-written poem is very much appreciated. He admires a picture in which she is in Indian attire with a loving smile. He feels sorry for such a vibrant lady. He has heard a lot about her personality and lively nature from his late wife Megha.

Her strong personality is reflected when she unfolds the mystery of Megha's death. Mayur always needs someone like her as a life partner. She is just a mirror image of her sister Megha- same enthusiasm, same loving nature and same captivating charm. He is admiring her eternal beauty and accepts if there is anyone who can replace Megha is none but Smriti. He knows whatever he is thinking will never be possible. Smriti is a mother of a child. Loss of Samar and second pregnancy can be handled only with the emotional support of family members. Time will heal her but how much time she will take is uncertain. He is not in hurry and patiently waiting for her to come out from the trauma. He has given Smriti all his contact details so that unhesitantly she can talk to him anytime. He feels extremely responsible towards her and Sunny.

One evening Samar finds his mother in a thoughtful mood as if she has something to share with Samar's father. Since his untimely death, the parents look more tensed. Her hesitation is reflected on her face but she is sure of having a discussion with her husband. While sipping herbal green tea she says, "Listen, I am worried about Smriti's future. Samar's death has broken all of us completely. I don't think I can overcome this shock. Before my death, I wish to fulfill my desire. Remember how desperately we wanted a daughter?

She takes a pause when finds her husband looking at her in a curious way. She continues, "We have now Smriti as our daughter. Can we get her remarried and do all rituals as her own parents? "

Mr. Chakraborty, Samar's father never expects this proposal from his wife. He surprisingly utters, "I have never realized you are such a progressive-minded lady. You are not a typical mother-in-law very strictly imposes restrictions on a widowed daughter-in-law. I am proud of you."

But soon he expresses his doubts related to the reaction of society. He says, "What will happen when people will criticize our modern thought? It can never be our sole decision. Smriti and her parents should agree and the next hurdle will be finding a bridegroom for a pregnant widow having one child already."

Mrs. Chakraborty assures him not to worry as she knows who will be the right man for Smriti. He again gives her a curious look and instantly asks if Mayur is in her mind. She responds positively. He seems happy but again creates doubt regarding Mayur's parents.

"Will they accept Smriti?" he looks worried.

"I don't know but if Mayur insists they can," she replies.

"Who will take the initiative? This is a sensitive issue. We have to be careful enough not to hurt anyone's sentiments. What about Smriti? Will she be ready to give Samar's place to Mayur?" He again utters.

"I shall discuss with Smriti's parents. Only they can convince her," she says.

Smriti's parents and brother are staying at Samar's house for a month so that Smriti won't feel alone. Though her in-laws are always with her in presence of own parents and sibling, she can restore her former strength little fast.

Late evening after dinner they all sit together on the terrace. Smriti is not with them as she needs rest.

Mrs. Chakraborty begins, "Samar's father is very tensed and in extreme fear when thinks about Smriti's future. How will she manage a business, her job, and her kids alone? We're at the ripened age. She must need a life partner. But who'll mentally prepare her for this?"

Mrs. Iyer, Smriti's mother can't believe that Mrs. Chakraborty is so concerned about the loneliness of her daughter-in-law. In India, it is common for a widower to remarry soon after the death of his wife, but for a widow even today it's a sin to think about it. The in-laws too never wish to proceed in this direction.

She asks if Mrs. Chakraborty has someone in her mind as after marriage Smriti belongs to them more than her biological parents.

Mrs. Chakraborty without wasting time utters, "Mayur."

The name spells magic on everyone. Instantly all agree. Mrs. Iyer hugs her and in sobbed voice declares she is a kind-hearted lady. She will set a positive example in society to follow.

The well-wishers of Smriti are now united to bring her out from this pain. The real problem is consent from Mayur's parents. Mrs. Iyer takes this responsibility. She will definitely convince them as Smriti is their darling.

While listening to this conversation Samar is shedding tears of joy. Mayur will surely be proved not only an understanding husband but also a responsible father of his kids. He is sincerely waiting for his wife's acceptance of the proposal. Before getting approval from Mayur's parents it is important how sincerely Mayur wants Smriti. To know the secret of Mayur's heart Samar visits his house. He gets a glimpse of Mayur's love for Smriti when finds him praying to God to fulfill his desire of having Smriti as his wife. Samar is glad. He doesn't find anything wrong desiring this. Both are bereft of their partners in their mid-35 and so both have the right to think about the new beginning of their life.

Samar knows Smriti has been mentally prepared for his early death since the prediction of the saint and thus is capable of raising two children singlehandedly. But he doesn't want her to sacrifice her life and live a widow's pathetic life who has none to wipe tears in deep agony. It's his responsibility of providing her love, care, and support. In his absence, she must have someone who can keep her happy. She must choose Mayur to lead a blessed married life.

He knows it is not so easy as both love their first love with heart and soul. he leaves everything in God's hands. Smriti is blessed to have such loving and caring people in her life. Her parents and brother together with Samar's parents are trying their best to keep her stress-free and prepare her to look ahead in the future.

Samar recalls the words of the saint he has met at Hampi. He thinks this is the right time to ask for a wish which will be granted by God. He closes his eyes and utters, "God, If I have done nothing wrong in my life; if I have been a dutiful son, husband, and father; if I have never hurt other's sentiments then do me a favor. Let Smriti and Mayur unite together as life partners."

At the breakfast table, in presence of entire family members, Mrs. Chakraborty says in a heavy voice, "How will Smriti live life without a life partner? Sunny must need a father to get emotional assistance. It will be hard to accept for the children that they are bereft of the father."

Mrs. Iyer agrees. Smriti just listens and before leaving the dining room she clears with her gestures that she is not ready to fulfill their desire. She can raise children single-handedly and will try her best to be both of the parents. If she is destined to live alone without any partner, then there is no guarantee second marriage will run long. She refuses to be a victim of bad luck once again. She narrates to them the prediction of the saint and requests not to repeat the topic of her second marriage again.

In Mayur's family, his mother is overjoyed after noticing a positive change in her son. His humor, love for music and his laughter are back. She has understood it is the impact of Smriti. She is determined to have Smriti at home as her daughter-in-law.

One day while applying oil on Mayur's head she asks him if he is ready to marry a widow having a son and is currently pregnant. He looks at her surprisingly because she will exercise her absolute right to reject any such proposal for him in no time without bothering his consent. But here is a different scenario. If mom is asking means she has already selected a lady. He asks her name and she says, "Smriti."

Mayur jumps with joy and hugs her tightly. "How do you know I want to marry her?" He asks.

"I am your mother knowing you since your fetus days. I can sense how your visit to Smriti's house has partially erased painful memories of Megha's death from your life. You look refresh. So your papa and I have decided that you should marry her."

"What about the approval of her family members? Who'll talk to her parents and in-laws? Further, I am unsure about her. I don't know if she'll allow me to take Samar's place in her life. What about Sunny? Will he accept me as his father?" Mayur has so many doubts running in his mind.

"Where there is a will there is a way, Son. I shall check if her parents want her to get settled down again? If I find even the slightest ray of hope, believe me, I will convince them to choose you as son–in–law. "

Mayur is perplexed. He is still unable to believe that his parents are so supportive and understanding. He wishes to have Smriti as a friend first. He wants to earn the love of Sunny. He unveils his heart in front of his parents. They agree instantly.

8
A NEW BEGINNING

After a monthiversary of Samar's death, Smriti shifts to her parents' home in Kerala till the birth of the child, for in Mumbai Samar's memories don't let her overcome the pain of the loss and her sadness may have a negative and inverse effect on the unborn. In Kerala, she is concentrating on her mental health as well as the development of both the children. Her parents and siblings try their best to create stress-free moments and keep her engage with light activities. Yoga class, membership of a library, a collection of her favorite movies and music albums, and pamper by family members show positive results. Her smile is back.

One evening Mayur and his parents pay a surprise visit to her home. They are gladly welcomed by the Iyer family. Mayur is relieved to see that Smriti has regained the glow on her face. She is in a light blue maternity gown, looking gorgeous. She joins them but after an hour goes to attend her yoga class. In her absence, the topic of discussion is her safe delivery and later her wedding with Mayur. Marriage is confirmed but her consent is still pending. It is in Mayur's hand how to sow seeds of love in Smriti's heart because without closing the last chapter it is impossible to write a new page of life.

Responsibility for Sunny's outdoor activities and Smriti's doctor's visit is taken by Mayur as he has taken transfer to the Kerala branch of his office for a year. He is residing with his parents in the company's flat which is near Smriti's residence. He has opted for work from home so that he can be with Smriti in hours of need. He is her 3 AM friend. Slowly, they become best buddies. The pain of the sudden loss of partners has united them. Both fill the vacuum of their life with each other's company. Their loneliness is now a thing of the past. Smriti is so amazed to get Mayur around her whenever she needs in spite of his busy schedule. She too begins to understand him and taking care of him.

One night, Smriti goes to bed early. Samar appears in her dream because the only medium to connect is through her dream. He is concerned about her safety and life-long happiness. He holds her hand and with much love in his eyes pleads her to start her life anew with Mayur. Smriti denies. She has loved Samar and in this life, she can't think of giving his place to Mayur in her heart. Samar insists. He says if she remains single, his soul won't get rest in peace. He requests her to remarry for the sake of the children. He assures that Mayur loves her as much as he does. He has seen how serious Mayur is in starting life with her and her children.

She wakes up at the ringing of her phone. The moon is shining in the sky. It's 11 PM. She gulps water and picks up the phone as the call is of her mother-in-law. What happens? Is everything fine? She is so panic-stricken. Mrs. Chakraborty calms her down and informs her she is visiting Kerala with Samar's father as in Mumbai they feel lonely. Smriti is so happy to hear it. She tells her about

Mayur's presence in Kerala. Samar's mother is relieved to hear Mayur is around Smriti. She feels as if her Samar is in front of her as Mayur. She has accepted from bottom of her heart Mayur as her son.

The next morning, at the breakfast table the entire family tries to convince Smriti to give herself a second chance. She is surprised. How everyone can suggest the same name "Mayur"? Is it God's indication? She remains silent and sits with Sunny to help him in his study. Sunny is no more an innocent kid. His father's death has matured him instantly.

He asks, "Mom, when will the little baby come?'

Smriti answers, "At the end of the year, son."

"Mom, will we go to Mumbai with the baby next year?"

"Yes, beta. With the little baby, we all will go back to our home. But why are you asking this?"

"Mom, Papa is not with us. But don't worry. I shall take care of you and the baby. I'll never demand anything to buy for me. My old toys can be used for the little baby. When I grow up, I shall also earn money and support you."

Smriti is stunned. A five- year old boy is worried about household expenses and is sacrificing his desires. She hugs him tightly and utters, "No son. You don't have to worry. Mummy will try her best to provide you and your sibling whatever you need. Papa has left us but he has made arrangements for all of us. There is no financial crunch. Please don't take the stress."

Sunny further asks, Mom, can't we stay with Mayur uncle? I love his company. I have noticed just like Papa he takes good care of us."

Smriti has nothing to say. She concentrates on teaching him some basic arithmetic rules. At that time her phone rings. She attends the call. It is Mayur. A formal conversation starts.

After a while, very hesitantly Mayur discloses his parent's wish. He says that they are waiting impatiently for her approval. She too tells him how Sunny finds a reflection of Samar in him and how much pressure to remarry is created by her family members and in-laws. She takes a pause and says," Last night Samar appeared in a dream and requested me to choose you as a father of my children. He thinks you can take his place and love his family as your own."

Mayur is taken aback. Without wasting time, he disconnects the phone and appears in front of her. In presence of everyone, he proposes to her. He asks if she is ready to hold his hand for her entire life because he loves her dearly and will treat her children as his own lifetime. At a certain age, partners are required for emotional assistance. He is sure they two are perfect for each other. She accepts his proposal. A year later, in a family courtroom Mayur and Smriti sign papers to be husband and wife legally. Their family is complete. They move to Canada. Smriti's second child is a baby girl. She resembles her father absolutely.

Is Samar reborn? No, his pious feeling and good deeds have liberated his soul from the eternal cycle of birth and rebirth. He has attained salvation. In Vaikuntha, he enjoys the ultimate bliss. He is an angel now. Love is eternal bliss. Unconditional love is powerful enough to raise a human being to the height of divinity. Smriti - Samar's love story has rekindled faith in true love. As an angel, Samar showers blessings on his family and is ever protective.

Time flies. Sunny and Samaira are teenagers now. They visit India once a year to meet their grandparents on Samar's death anniversary. Their arrival is celebrated jointly by Samar's, Smriti's, and Mayur's parents in a grand way. They all stay together to create beautiful memories. Smriti and Mayur feel blessed to have such a lovely family which is free from hypocrisy. They belong to the older generation but their progressive thinking gives strength to their children to live life without any inhibition and guilt. Samar is ever-present as it is believed those who love family never leave it.

Author's Biography

Aaradhana Agarwal has been penning her emotions since her school-going days. A literary family background and Masters in English literature have enhanced her writing skill. She is a novelist, poet, and story writer. Renowned newspapers have published her write-ups and in many writing competitions, she has been admired by the readers as well as the judges. As a co-author, she has participated in many anthologies.

She is a nature lover and very sensitive to others' pain as well as delight. She is a traveler and loves to capture nature's beauty. Books, movies, and music soothe her, and Bollywood songs are her favorite.

She is a teacher by profession and so very logical, practical in her approach towards life and she hates lies. She is a keen observer and a sharp thinker and doesn't live in the past. She admits situations in reality without any beautiful coating of falsehood and reveals the hardcore truth in her creations. She is a Podcaster and a You Tuber

Her poems, stories are played on the radio. Listeners and readers find hope, love for life in her writings. She has authored the following books:

1. 1. Tangible Abstracts (an e-book on poems)
   2. Love – Life's Rainbow (an e-book on love stories)
   3. Tendrils – An Attachment (an e-book on women-oriented short stories)
   4. Dispersed Petals (a collection of short stories)
   5. Warmth of Sunshine (a collection of short stories)
   6. A Masterpiece (a collection of short stories)
   7. The Wheel of Fortune (a collection of short stories)

AUTHOR'S BIOGRAPHY

8. Rhythm of Life (a collection of short stories)

9. Bhaavnaao ka vistrit samandar (a collection of Hindi poems)

10. A Roar of Silence (a collection of poems)

11-Lockdown (a collection of English and Hindi poems)

12-And a new journey begins (a collection of stories)

13- A SIP OF TEA (an English novel)

14- A FORBIDDEN NIGHTINGALE (a collection of English stories)

15- THE LAST PRAYER (An English novel e-book)

CPSIA information can be obtained
at www.ICGtesting.com
Printed in the USA
LVHW090553250122
709218LV00008B/653